An Octopus Followed Me Home

Dan Yaccarino

PUFFIN BOOKS

PUFFIN BOOKS
Published by the Penguin Group
Penguin Putnam Books for Young Readers, 345 Hudson Street, New York, New York 10014, U.S.A.
Penguin Books Ltd, 27 Wrights Lane, London W8 5TZ, England
Penguin Books Australia Ltd, Ringwood, Victoria, Australia
Penguin Books Canada Ltd, 10 Alcorn Avenue, Toronto, Ontario, Canada M4V 3B2
Penguin Books (N.Z.) Ltd, 182-190 Wairau Road, Auckland 10, New Zealand

Penguin Books Ltd, Registered Offices: Harmondsworth, Middlesex, England

First published in the United States of America by Viking, a member of Penguin Putnam Inc., 1997
Published by Puffin Books, a member of Penguin Putnam Books for Young Readers, 2000

1 3 5 7 9 10 8 6 4 2

THE LIBRARY OF CONGRESS HAS CATALOGED THE VIKING EDITION AS FOLLOWS:
Yaccarino, Dan.
An octopus followed me home / by Dan Yaccarino.   p.   cm.
Summary: When a girl brings home an octopus and wants to keep him as a pet, her daddy reminds her
of the crocodile, seals, and other inappropriate animals she has already brought into the house to create chaos.
ISBN 0-670-87401-9
[1. Animals—Fiction. 2. Pets—Fiction. 3. Stories in rhyme.] I. Title. PZ8.3.Y24On 1997 [E]—dc21 97-8821 CIP AC

Puffin Books ISBN 0-14-056532-9

Printed in the United States of America

For Terry and Scooter

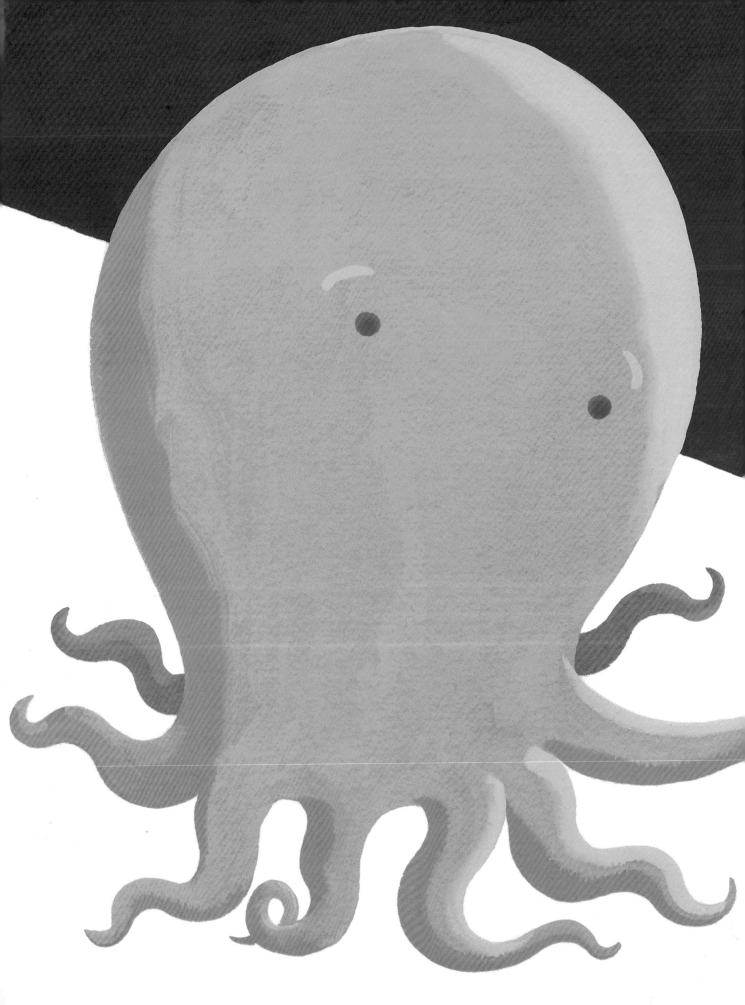

An octopus followed me home today,
One that I promise to love.

Can we keep him? Can he stay?

I'll teach him to sleep in the tub.

"I'd like to remind you," my daddy said,

"Of all the pets I let you keep.

"Like the crocodile who lives under my bed

And won't let me get any sleep.

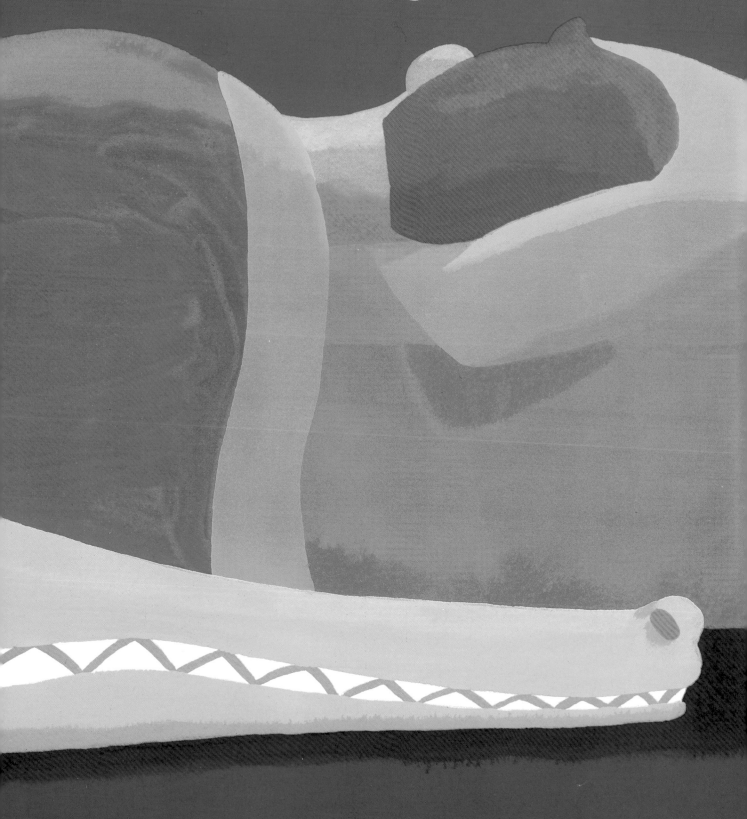

"Or the pesky seals who float about,

So I can't even swim in my pool.

"And the long-necked giraffe
who sticks his head out

Whenever you go off to school.

"Then there's the grizzly bear we took in.

I hope he keeps hibernating.

"And what about those penguins?
They all need refrigerating!

**"Not to mention those mountain goats
Who haven't come down since May.**

"But it's those rabbits I hate the most. They multiply every day!

**"This morning, I couldn't believe my eyes—
I thought it must be a mirage—**

**When all of a sudden I realized
I now had a two-elephant garage!**

"Now this is too much," Dad said. "No more!

You return that octopus right now!

"That's the last pet to come through this door.

Not another rhino, tiger, or cow!"

We waved good-bye and felt so sad—

He seemed so lost and alone.

But he'll be okay,
and I don't feel too bad . . .
Since another pet
followed me home!